Property of
West Jackson Middle School

MANCHESTER UNITED

BY
MARK STEWART

NORWOODHOUSE PRESS

Chicago, Illinois

NORWOOD HOUSE 🏠 PRESS

P.O. Box 316598 • Chicago, Illinois 60631
For more information about Norwood House Press please visit our website at
www.norwoodhousepress.com or call 866-565-2900.

Photography and Collectibles:
The trading cards and other memorabilia assembled in the background for this book's cover and interior pages are all part of the author's collection and are reproduced for educational and artistic purposes.

All photos courtesy of Associated Press except the following individual photos and artifacts (page numbers): F.K.S. Publishers Ltd. (6), Author's Collection (10 top), Country & Sporting Publications Ltd. (10 bottom), Brooke Bond Ltd. (11 top), LFP/Panini (11 middle), The Upper Deck Company LLC (11 bottom, 16), Wolff Evans/MUFC (22).

Cover image: Simon Bellis/Associated Press

Designer: Ron Jaffe
Series Editor: Mike Kennedy
Content Consultants: Michael Jacobsen, Ben Gould and Jonathan Wentworth-Ping
Project Management: Black Book Partners, LLC
Editorial Production: Lisa Walsh

LIBRARY OF CONGRESS CATALOGING-IN-PUBLICATION DATA
Names: Stewart, Mark, 1960 July 7- author.
Title: Manchester United / by Mark Stewart.
Description: Chicago Illinois : Norwood House Press, 2017. | Series: First
   touch soccer | Includes bibliographical references and index.
Identifiers: LCCN 2016058988 (print) | LCCN 2017015222 (ebook) | ISBN
   9781684040797 (eBook) | ISBN 9781599538600 (library edition : alk. paper)
Subjects: LCSH: Manchester United (Soccer team)--History--Juvenile
   literature.
Classification: LCC GV943.6.M3 (ebook) | LCC GV943.6.M3 S48 2018 (print) |
   DDC 796.334/630942733--dc23
LC record available at https://lccn.loc.gov/2016058988

This publication is intended for educational purposes and is not affiliated with any team, league, or association including: Manchester United Football Club, the English Premier League, The Union of European Football Associations (UEFA), or the Federation Internationale de Football Association (FIFA).

302N--072017
Manufactured in the United States of America in North Mankato, Minnesota.

CONTENTS

Words in **bold type** are defined on page 24.

Wayne Rooney has a big grin after scoring in a 2016 match. Teammate Juan Mata is the first to congratulate him.

Meet Manchester United

The city of Manchester is one of the oldest in England. Its most successful team is the Manchester United Football Club. In most parts of the world, when people say "football" they are talking about the game of soccer, not American football.

Fans call Manchester United "ManU" for short. They nicknamed the players The Red Devils. They play to win, but also play to have fun.

TIME MACHINE

In 1878, railroad workers in the Newton Heath section of Manchester formed a soccer team. They called themselves the Heathens. In 1902, the team changed its name to Manchester United. Between 1908 and 2013, the club won 20 league championships. Its great stars include Jack Rowley, **Bobby Charlton**, George Best, and Ryan Giggs.

Ryan Giggs takes the ball away from an opponent during a 2004 match.

There is no place a ManU fan would rather be than in the stands at Old Trafford.

Best Seat in the House

Manchester United plays in one of soccer's most famous stadiums. It was built in 1910 and holds more than 75,000 fans. They call the stadium Old Trafford. Bobby Charlton once called it the "theater of dreams" because every young player has dreamed of playing there. In 2006, many new touches were added to Old Trafford.

COLLECTOR'S CORNER

These collectibles show some of the best Manchester United players ever.

COPE'S "CLIPS"

No. 125—MEREDITH
Manchester United
Noted Footballers

BILLY MEREDITH

Forward
1906–1921
Meredith was one of soccer's first great one-on-one players. He often drew three or four defenders.

ROGER BYRNE

Fullback
1951–1958
Byrne's tough defense helped ManU win three league titles. He and seven other teammates died in a plane crash in 1958.

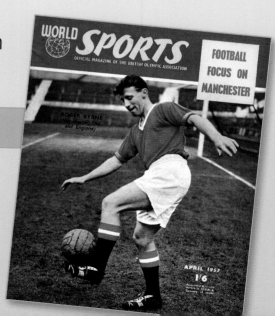

WORLD SPORTS
OFFICIAL MAGAZINE OF THE BRITISH OLYMPIC ASSOCIATION

FOOTBALL FOCUS ON MANCHESTER

ROGER BYRNE
(Manchester, Eng.
and England)

APRIL 1957
1/6

DAVID BECKHAM

Forward
1992–2003
Fans at Old Trafford still talk about Beckham's amazing passes and long shots. He once scored a goal from the halfway line.

RYAN GIGGS

Midfielder
1990–2014
Giggs played more games for ManU than anyone else. He scored 168 goals in 963 matches.

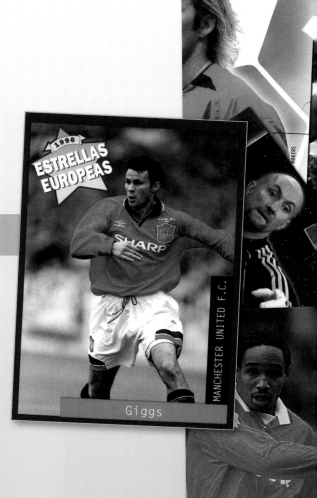

Giggs

MANCHESTER UNITED F.C.

PAUL SCHOLES

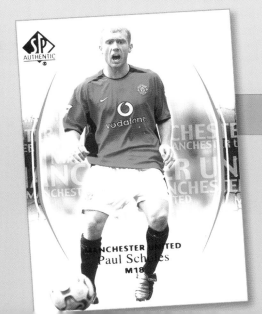

Midfielder
1992–2013
Many believe that Scholes was the club's best midfielder ever. He never got tired and rarely made a bad pass or play.

WORTHY OPPONENTS

Manchester United has two very old rivals. One is Manchester City, a club that plays about 15 minutes away. They have met more than 170 times. Their games are called the Manchester Derby. Another rival is Liverpool. Manchester United and Liverpool are two of England's best clubs. They play less than an hour apart.

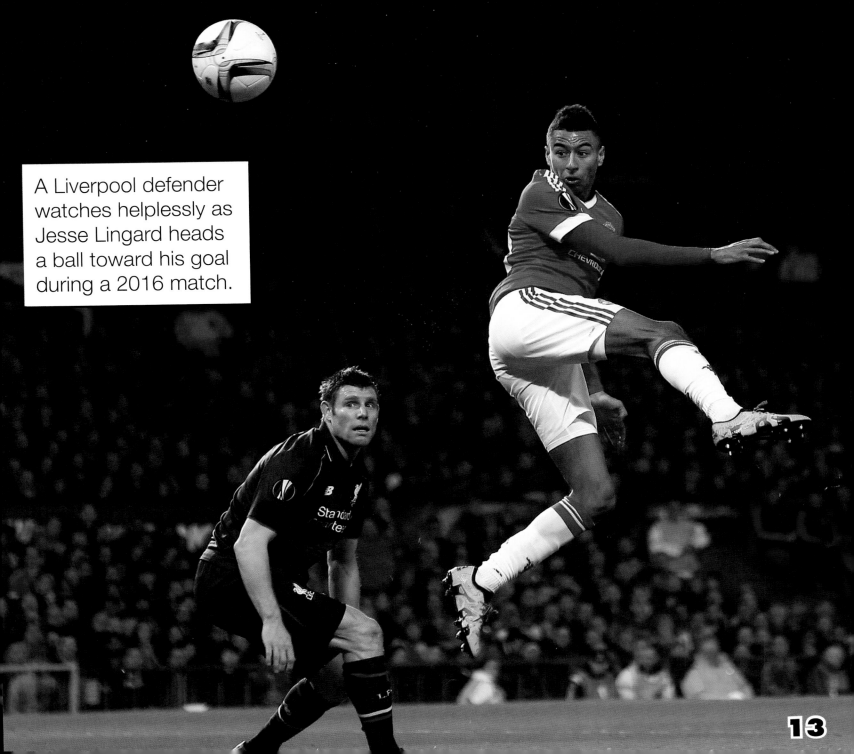

A Liverpool defender watches helplessly as Jesse Lingard heads a ball toward his goal during a 2016 match.

CLUB WAYS

Each Friday before a match, Manchester United players help themselves to a bowl of toffee pudding. The tradition began after Ruud van Nistelrooy tried the sweet, sticky dessert and scored three goals the next day. Many fans also eat a "player dessert" the day before a Saturday match. Those who do not like toffee pudding might try apple crumble and custard.

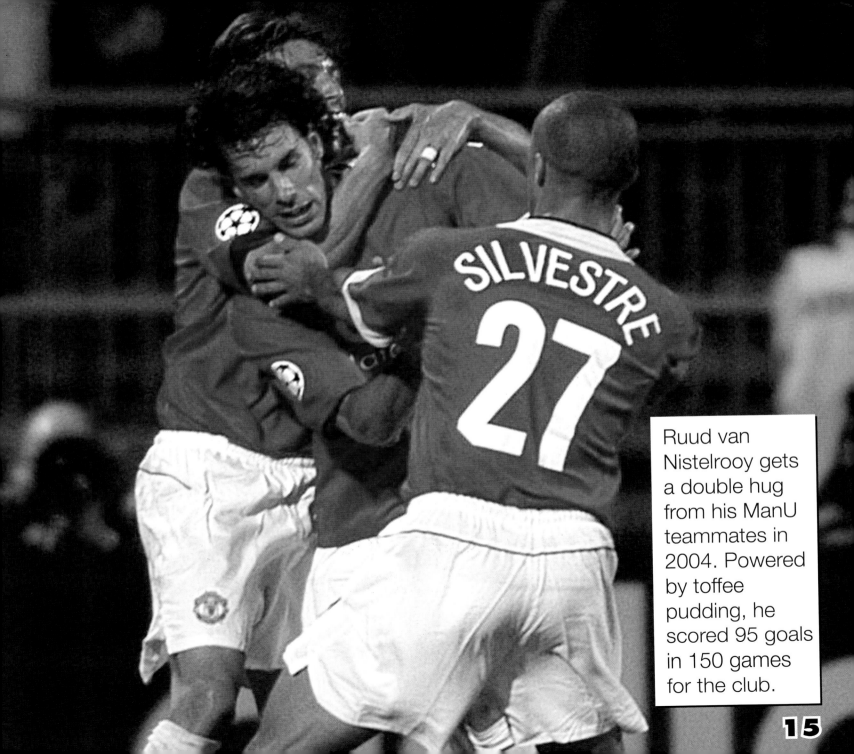

Ruud van Nistelrooy gets a double hug from his ManU teammates in 2004. Powered by toffee pudding, he scored 95 goals in 150 games for the club.

ON THE MAP

Manchester United brings together players from many countries. These are some of the best:

1 **Eric Cantona** • Marseille, France

2 **Peter Schmeichel** • Gladsaxe, Denmark

3 **Ruud van Nistelrooy** • Oss, Netherlands

4 **Juan Mata** • Burgos, Spain

5 **Park Ji-sung** • Goheung, South Korea

6 **Tim Howard** • North Brunswick, New Jersey, USA

7 **Dwight Yorke** • Trinidad and Tobago

8 **Antonio Valencia** • Lago Agrio, Ecuador

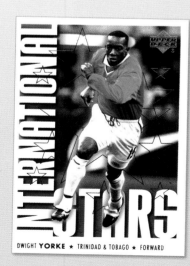

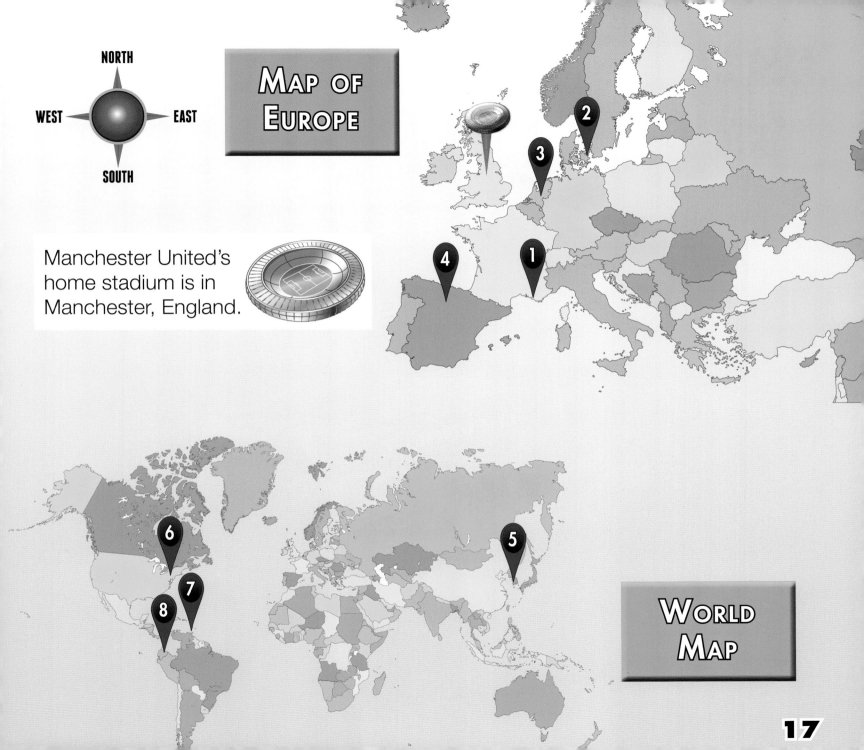

NORTH

WEST ● EAST

SOUTH

MAP OF EUROPE

Manchester United's home stadium is in Manchester, England.

WORLD MAP

17

Wayne Rooney models Manchester United's home kit. The club crest can be seen on his chest.

KIT AND CREST

Manchester United players wear red shirts, white shorts, and black socks for most home games. The away kit includes a white shirt, black shorts, and white socks. Sometimes when ManU is the visiting team, it will wear different colors if the home team has a similar uniform. The club's crest shows a sailing ship and a devil.

WE WON!

In 1998–99, ManU finished first in England's **Premier League**. It also won the FA Cup, the top tournament in English soccer. Later that season, the club reached the final of the **Champions League**. The Red Devils trailed Bayern Munich 1–0 with three minutes to go. David Beckham set up the tying and winning goals with perfect **corner kicks** for an amazing victory.

Manchester United manager Alex Ferguson is surrounded by his players after winning the 1999 Champions League.

FOR THE RECORD

ManU has won more than 30 championships!

Football League/Premier League

20 championships
(from 1907–08 to 2012–13)

European Cup/Champions League

1967–68, 1998–99 & 2007–08

FA Cup

12 championships
(from 1908–09 to 2015–16)

European Super Cup

1991

Cup Winners' Cup

1990–91

Intercontinental Cup

1999

FIFA Club World Cup

2008

George Best

These players have won major awards while playing for Manchester United:

1964 Denis Law • European Footballer of the Year

1966 Bobby Charlton • European Footballer of the Year

1968 George Best • European Footballer of the Year

1996 Peter Schmeichel • Premier League Player of the Season

1999 Dwight Yorke • Premier League Player of the Season

1999 David Beckham • European Footballer of the Year

2003 Ruud van Nistelrooy • Premier League Player of the Season

2007 Cristiano Ronaldo • Premier League Player of the Season

2008 Cristiano Ronaldo • Premier League Player of the Season

2008 Cristiano Rolando • European Footballer of the Year

2008 Cristiano Ronaldo • World Player of the Year

2009 Nemanja Vidic • Premier League Player of the Season

2010 Wayne Rooney • Premier League Player of the Season

2011 Nemanja Vidic • Premier League Player of the Season

Soccer Words

Champions League
A tournament among the top clubs in Europe. The competition was called the European Cup until 1992.

Corner Kicks
Free kicks given to the attacking team after the ball crosses the goal line, having been touched last by a defending player.

Premier League
England's top soccer league.

Index

Photos are on **BOLD** numbered pages.

About the Author

Mark Stewart has been writing about world soccer since the 1990s, including *Soccer: A History of the World's Most Popular Game*. In 2005, he co-authored Major League Soccer's 10-year anniversary book.

About Manchester United

Learn more at these websites:
www.manutd.com
www.fifa.com
www.teamspiritextras.com